SALLY'S CLOSET

A Story of Secrets, Sadness and Self-Discovery

SALLY'S CLOSET

A Story of Secrets, Sadness and Self-Discovery

Rev. Janice Chrysler, CH

Rev. Janice Chrysler, CH
https://mindfuljourney.ca

ISBN 978-0-9949831-4-5 (Paperback)
ISBN 978-0-9949831-5-2 (eBook)
ISBN 978-0-9949831-6-9 (Audiobook)

Edited by B. Arden Services
Cover Illustration by Christina Chrysler
Book production and design by Dawn James,
Publish and Promote
Perseus Design, Cover, Interior Layout & Design

The information in this book is not intended as a substitute for medical or professional advice. It is strictly the opinion of the author. It is recommended that you consult your professional healthcare provider if you have any physical, mental, or emotional health concerns.

Printed and bound in Canada

I would like to thank all the family, friends and clients who have opened their hearts and bared their souls to me over the years. I am truly blessed for having the opportunity to hold sacred space with you. I have learned more from you than you may ever realize, and I give thanks to the Divine that by working together you were able to step out of your darkness and into your own beautiful light.

To my loving and supportive husband Monty, our two children Ernie and Christina and grandchildren Owen and Ellie, thank you for being there for me and loving me and my offbeat ways. Then there are my Soul Sisters, Valla, Katharine, Darcelle and Laurane. Together we have solved some interesting problems, come up with some amazing ideas and are continuously working on being the most awesome crones of consciousness out there! You all remind me to laugh, live and love. And last but never least, hugs and thanks to my loving mother, who at 94, still has my back and is my biggest fan. Blessings to all of you and thank you for being part of my life.

Contents

Preface

Growing up I was blessed with a family and a home where I always felt safe and loved. Some of my best memories are of the times I spent alone in my room playing with my dolls, dishes and books. There was always a tea party to get dressed up for, a doll to push in a carriage, and books to pretend to read to my classroom of stuffed teddy bears and monkeys. Then when my older brothers were at school, I would quietly go on an adventure in the forbidden land of their bedroom. If I was lucky, I would be able to look through all their toys and things before my mother came looking for me. Every day held something new to learn, whether it was helping my mother bake, learning to ride my bike, playing catch with my Dad or walking in the woods. Life was simple and easy....then, came school!

Life seemed to change dramatically when I had to pack that lunch box and walk off to school. I was so excited to go and learn to read my books and spell my name. I didn't realize how different it would be from being at home. No more playing all day or having time alone, or even being able to get a hug from my Mom when I was feeling scared of the other kids. Looking back, I realize I was bullied by a few of the children. I wasn't sure how to handle it but I just did. I tucked all the memories away in the back of my mind and focused on other things. After all, I was a girl and a girl in the '60s was expected to act a certain way. If the boys were picking on me it must be something I was doing right? Boy has my attitude on that one changed!

Time went on as it does; I grew up like other children do and began to make up my own mind about life or at least was trying to figure it out. Like so many people I didn't realize when we hide things inside they can grow and fester into fears and in turn those fears can stop us from being our true authentic selves. Opportunities can be missed from the fear of trying something new, what others will think or say or in making a mistake. At a very young age I knew I would be doing something spiritual with my life but of course, had no idea what that might be. I would lie in bed trying to get my head wrapped around life and death, right and wrong, eternity, and what to wear to school the next day. Then throw in a changing body, boys and dating. Wow! Talk about ups and downs and life tossed around.

I was fortunate to have support at home but as I grew, I soon realized that not every home was safe, not every couple were in love, not every woman was respected and not every man could be trusted. There were people who pretended to be your friend but really used you. Some people would walk beside you, others would follow and there were those who claimed to support you but ran away when times were tough. Every day seemed to bring changes, both enjoyable and heart-breaking. Tears flowed from both laughter and sadness, and often within a few short moments of one another. This growing up was not easy!

There was one thing that would always calm everything down. I remember the peaceful feeling I would get when the moon was full and I would open my curtains and let it cascade over my bed. At the time I had no idea of the moon's energy, only that I felt the world slip away as I drifted off to sleep. Even today, I find the full moon the most peaceful time of the month and try to sit in its radiance whenever I can.

Throughout my teens and adult years, I seemed to be a magnet for those looking to share their innermost secrets. I began to understand how storing away things from our past eventually builds up until we can no longer cope either physically or emotionally or both.

I now look back on my own life experiences and those of others kindly shared with me and give thanks for the lessons I have learned from all of them. It has given me my drive to work with organizations that support women's rights and to those providing healing work for the survivors of sexual abuse and domestic violence. My spiritual work comes in all forms by holding sacred space for others where they too can heal.

When we share our stories instead of keeping secrets we not only heal ourselves but we hold out a hand for someone else to heal as well. When we face our fears instead of pretending they do not exist we take away the fear's power of keeping us in sadness. When we realize that we have the choice about what thoughts we keep and what ones we let go, we create our own reality. When we choose to live in love, we are then able to let go of the secrets and sadness and open ourselves to begin the journey of self-discovery.

Introduction

Oh, the innocence of a young girl named Sally! Perhaps her story will remind you of when you were little playing with your toys and letting your imagination run wild. Maybe you can relate to her experiences as she matures and moves through the growing pains that life can throw in her path. What choices are to be made along the way?

What if we were like Sally and could have a closet that would hold all our memories? Would we be able to store everything, absolutely everything in that closet? Would we want to? Like all things we tend to gather, there will come a time when there is simply too much "stuff" and something has to be done. After all, how many times can we push and shove, stack and pile things in the closet before it overflows?

Well, Sally tries to do just that, but over time finds what used to be easy to do as a young child, becomes more difficult as she gets older. There are times of sadness which consume her and dark secrets fed by fears which constantly lurk just inside her closet doors. Sally has decisions to make but like a lot of us, puts them off, ignores them or simply pretends they do not exist. If things don't go right there is always someone or something to blame. After all, how important can all these things actually be?

Sally, like us, goes through life holding onto things that she no longer needs without realizing how much they are weighing her down. Way back in the cell memory of her subconscious mind, fears are feeding her ego and stopping her from taking chances, making changes and opening up to truly be all she can be. Sally lives under the illusion that she can hide behind a smile and all will be well.

How often do we travel through life allowing our fears to guide us? Have opportunities been turned down out of the fear of taking a chance? Did we hold back on speaking and living our truth out of fear of what others may think? Were there times we felt afraid because of some abuse from our childhood? Do we allow our minds to be filled with other people's ideas? So many things to think about or ignore. What would you choose?

Perhaps you are on a similar road yourself and are feeling a little lost. There is hope and tools you can use to free yourself from the heavy burden you are carrying. Follow Sally as she makes a major discovery through her own story of secrets, sadness and self-discovery.

Chapter One

The Innocence

Once upon a time, many years ago, in a place not far away, lived a lovely little girl named Sally. Her most favourite place in the whole wide world was her bedroom. It was here that she played with her dolls, built kingdoms with her blocks and traveled to make-believe places through her books. Happiness came naturally to Sally as she played, laughed, giggled, sang and danced alone in her room. Not a worry in the world because she felt she could be herself and do anything here in her special place. After all, Sally never thought of being anything else but happy!

But the best part of being in her room came just before sleep when she would tiptoe over to her window, slowly drawback her curtains and gaze out at the moon and all the twinkling stars in the sky. Sally could look at the universe forever it seemed. There couldn't possibly be anything more magnificently wondrous than a night's sky. If she was lucky and the moon was full, Sally would push back the curtains until its glorious light shone right in on her bed. Then she would curl up in her big comfy bed where she would close her eyes tight, take a great big breath in and quietly whisper a wish. All the while, the light of the moon cascaded over her little body and gently soothed her to sleep. It was on these nights that Sally would dream dreamy dreams.

Sally would sometimes spend time all alone in her room just thinking....thinking about the fun she had that day at a friend's party, how nice her mommy's cookies tasted, how happy she felt when her daddy taught her to ride her bicycle or what great things she had learned that day at school. As she thought about these happy thoughts, she wondered how she would ever be able to remember them all. After all the world was new to Sally and it had so many things to teach her and she wanted to remember all the people she met, the adventures she went on and the conversations she had with people that day. That is when Sally had the greatest thought of all!

How wonderful for Sally that she appreciated all the beautiful things that happened in her day! Isn't it wonderful how children can be so content with their own company? They can play, sing, dance and laugh anywhere because they are simply being their authentic selves and living in that moment. Remember we were all children once too! When was the last time you danced like no one was watching? Have you sung lately at the top of your lungs, off-key or not, to a song on the radio or one in your head, using the right words or made some up? How many times have you walked in the rain, laughed in the sunshine or gazed at the beauty of the thousands of twinkling lights in the night sky? Have you ever invited the comforting light of a full moon to flow over you and to envelope you completely? Can you remember the touch of a summer's breeze or the kiss of the sun upon your face? Such simple everyday pleasures are just there for our taking, if only we would choose to embrace them and allow ourselves to be one with their greatness. Perhaps that is why children can find happiness; ignorance is truly bliss. As children, we did not look for anything but pleasure, love and compassion, and we were open to receive it.

Oh, the innocence of youth! Isn't it amazing how we all come into this world with a sense of wonderment and the desire to learn, explore and be all we can be? As beautiful beings of light, we had decided to come to this little blue planet to learn about living, gaining happiness, experiencing joy, compassion and hope. Without being told, we intuitively knew love and we sought ways to experience it. As infants, we depended on adults to nurture us not only physically but emotionally. We were comforted by our mother's caress and in times of want, a soothing voice and a gentle embrace was all that we needed to feel safe. We automatically felt a connection to the earth and enjoyed being out in nature; walking barefoot so we could feel the warmth of the earth and the softness of the grass beneath our feet, or cool mud oozing between our toes. Didn't we all collect rocks, often going through a handful to find the perfect one whether it was how it looked or how it felt in our hand? Many stones, sticks and even bugs were pushed deep into little pockets where their eventual fate would be to travel through the laundry cycle! What was more amazing than lying on the grass and gazing up into the clouds to see what forms took shape? What about catching snowflakes on our tongues, dancing in the rain or attempting to gather the swirling leaves in the wind and how this brought moments of laughter and joy. The simplest of life's experiences would become the greatest events of our day!

Over time some of us would be tree climbers, trailblazers and risk-takers while others would follow blindly, or some would decide to sit this one out to think it through a bit more. Sometimes these adventures would be shared with others and sometimes we would go through them all by ourselves. Regardless of what we did, it was all a life experience, something new for us at that moment in time. We seemed to realize that every day brought a new first time for something, and we accepted and embraced it.

As children our minds were like a sponge, taking in all the sights, sounds and happenings around us even if we didn't yet understand exactly what they all meant. We trusted what we experienced was life as it should be. Instinctively we came into this world longing for a sense of belonging to a tribe or group. Our families, culture, and the belief systems we were raised in, would over time contribute to how we interpreted these experiences and begin to shape our way of thinking. Without realizing it, we were developing a sense of right and wrong, good and evil, what was expected of us and what we could become. As children, we depended on those around us to bring light into our lives, to explain the world and shape our destiny.

When we first came into this little blue planet we had to go along with the tribe because we knew nothing else. We depended on our parents or guardians to keep us safe, to protect and nurture us. However, within our soul we knew we needed and deserved to be loved. Our actions were all about gaining love, feeling loved and giving love to others in order to gain a sense of security and belonging. At the core of all of us, then and today, is the desire to experience love in our life. Our personal opinion on how that should be expressed, received or given can go back to how it was presented to us when we were children. What memories did we hold onto? What actions of giving and receiving love and joy did we keep and use today?

Like Sally, we reached an age when we would try to get our head wrapped around the thought of growing up. After all, while we were pretending to be Barbie in a frogman suit in a spaceship filled with toy cars, dolls and cookies it was hard to imagine being anything else! Yet it seemed that every day we were learning something new and in fact, we were! How could we remember all these things until we were all grown up? It no doubt seemed an impossible task. Yet, without even realizing it our subconscious mind had already devised a plan to hold onto all these memories. Just like Sally, we knew that all our experiences were ours and ours alone and we would be the ones who decided what to do with them.

There was a time when we never worried about tomorrow because we didn't know anything but this moment in time. It wasn't until our family, culture and the belief system we were exposed to told us what to think, how to act, what was right and what was wrong. Then slowly the concept of time was woven into our lives and we developed a need to hold onto what we had just experienced. Without even realizing it, we were beginning to form judgments which in turn would shape our understanding of past, present and future.

Chapter Two

Life Happens

At the end of her room was a large wooden door that opened into an empty closet. The closet had lots and lots of shelves that went right from the floor to the ceiling. Sally could never decide what to put in there until now. She would make beautiful boxes to hold her special memories. So, with that thought in mind, Sally got right to work cutting and pasting, colouring and drawing then filling every box with a special memory. What a wonderful idea this was; just making the boxes made Sally very, very happy.

"There," Sally exclaimed as she smiled the biggest smile she could possibly make and placed the first box on the shelf, "now every time I open the

closet I will be reminded of how happy I felt when I made that box." Then Sally smiled even more as she realized just how happy she really did feel.

So it was, Sally would make a beautifully deco-rated box representing a special day in her life and place it lovingly on a shelf in her closet. Every time she would open the closet door, she would see all her boxes and smile to herself as she remembered the wonderful feelings each box contained. There were birthday boxes, holiday boxes, time with fam-ily and friends' boxes, school boxes, playing with her toys boxes, dancing in the rain boxes and well, just about everything sunny and bright boxes and of course, sleeping in the light of the moon boxes.

Then time went on, as time tends to do, and Sally grew older as little girls do. She soon learned not all memories are happy ones. Since so many of these emotions and life experiences were brand new to Sally, she decided perhaps she needed to keep these as well. However, when she felt angry, she was in no mood and in too big of a hurry to decorate the boxes with bright colours and bows. Instead, she would just open the door, shove the box inside, not even caring where it went and often slamming the door shut, "bang!" with the kick of her boot. Other times when Sally was sad, she tried desperately to hide those feelings in the darkest, plainest black or brown box she could find. This box too was just slid inside with the hope that it would disappear deep within the darkness of the closet. Sally found it was often difficult to let go of the sad boxes, especially if the sadness was heavy enough to make her cry. It was as though her tears melted the boxes in her hands. However, eventually she would put them away, closing the door by leaning against it, then releasing a heavy "sigh".

Sometimes she had emotions from experiences she couldn't even label because they were so new to her. Even though it was hard for Sally to understand what was going around her, deep inside her soul seemed to know that one day it would all make sense but right now into the closet it would go. What was going on with Sally? Where did her constant joy and happiness disappear to? Oh, it was still there most of the time but somehow things were different now. All too often Sally found herself feeling very confused, especially when someone she had trusted said or did something that hurt her emotionally.

There was the time when a man in her family whom she loved so much, began saying things to her she didn't understand and then did something to her body that made her feel very frightened. Why did he do this to her? He told her it was how girls were supposed to act and she was bad if she didn't. Sally had never felt bad or frightened like this before. Should she tell her parents? If not wanting to do these things and telling about them made her bad, Sally didn't want her parents to be angry too. The man had told her she was to be quiet about it... it was their secret and if she was good to him, he wouldn't tell her parents how bad she had been to try and stop him.

Sally was also being told by her tribe it was time for her to grow up, to act a certain way and even to think a certain way. This was all new to her. Maybe she had said or done something wrong and this man misunderstood; maybe she asked for his behavior without even realizing it! If she told her parents, who she loved to the moon and back, would they be angry with her for being so childish or worse would they be disappointed in her? As far as her family knew he was the good guy, buying her ice cream cones and volunteering to babysit. Sally soon realized not all secrets made you feel good, but she tucked this one away.

There were many times Sally wished she could go back to the days when all she needed to do was decorate her beautiful joy-filled boxes. Life seemed simpler when she was living in the moment but now she had to think about what to wear, where to go, what people to hang around with, and even what she was going to do when she was a grown-up. A grown-up? She didn't feel like she was being allowed to be a kid anymore. Even her own body was changing in ways that Sally couldn't comprehend. She was beginning to look at others and herself in more judgmental ways and often found herself feeling less than perfect. Sally was certain her friends and school mates were all talking about her, inspecting her every move and critiquing her clothes and even what she ate. One thing she did realize was there was no going back to the way things used to be because there were just too many things and decisions to make now.

What was going on with Sally? As she grew, she received love and joy from her family and allowed those feelings to bring her happiness. She busily decorated boxes and tucked them away in her closet so she would be able to open the door and take in all the beauty on the shelves whenever she wanted to. It seemed like such a wonderful idea at the time and really, it was. However, one of the biggest lessons we come to learn, and Sally soon did too, is that not all moments in this life are ones of joy and bliss. As a child, she couldn't even put a name on these emotions as they were brand new and perhaps even strange to her. Regardless, she boxed these up too and added them to her closet. Growing up is not easy but it is a journey we all take when we agree to come into this world. Sally didn't realize it but all her boxes were adding information to the cell memory of her data bank, better known as her subconscious.

When we come into this world, our main desire is to be loved and be part of a tribe. We put all our trust into their hands having faith that even if bad things happen, we have a place or people we can turn to who will protect and comfort us. The people and the culture around us shapes our thinking and perception of what is right and wrong, what we believe, how we should act, how we should be treated and what we should expect from others. After all, we have not known anything else up to this point in time on the planet. Those around us are shaping our thoughts, actions and reactions even if they are not totally aware of what they are doing. Those times when a member of our tribe does or says something to us that hurts us, breaks our trust or abuses us physically and emotionally we hold onto it. As a child, we don't know where to turn, where our voice will be heard or for that matter, we may not even know what to say! After all, when we were children we had no way of knowing if the treatment we were receiving was right or wrong but we do remember how it made us feel. Too often the abuser will use scare tactics to manipulate the child to keep them quiet. The child then feels it is their fault these things happen, or that they happen to all children and they must accept it. After all, who will listen? If they do tell will they be punished too? So, a secret is made and, in many cases, never gets spoken. The burden of carrying these secrets only gets heavier as the child ages, and it can manifest in so many areas of their life. It isn't until they can recall these situations through their adult eyes that they can see the harm that was done to them. But then what?

Our subconscious mind absorbs everything like a sponge without differentiating those actions and reactions that are positive or negative to our well being. It busily matches an experience and how we reacted emotionally and physically to that action. For example, if we were disciplined when very young for giving our opinion or asking questions, we may grow up being afraid of what others think of us. We may even feel our opinions and ideas are of lesser value than those of others. Without consciously being aware of this, we may deny ourselves the opportunities to speak up or offer our knowledge, because strong messages are going through our being from our subconscious memory bank of what happened when we were a child. We don't always, if ever, get the full memory but what we do receive is the feeling and the fear, so we remain quiet.

Our journey on this earth is like a huge roller coaster ride. There are times when we are squealing with delight and excitement, or we find ourselves gripping on out of fear for our very lives. Everyone on that roller coaster is experiencing the ride but how each person reacts is unique to them. So much will depend on what cell memory they have already stored away in their subconscious mind and what bits and pieces of this ride will be allowed to be added. At the end of the ride, everyone will share one thing in common and that is how it made them feel. Some will be happy, others afraid, but everyone will have some emotional attachment to this experience. Everything we do in life is like this. Our decision to even try something new can be attached to either pleasure or pain from a past experience similar to this one. We will move forward out of love or allow it to keep us a prisoner out of fear. This all happens so quickly that most of the time we don't even realize what is going on or why we are reacting the way we do. Like Sally, we rationalize that we don't have time to sort things out as we have so much to do, people to please, goals to reach, or we may believe we don't have any say in our own lives. It is then that our closet starts to get filled with thoughts, actions and opinions of others which over time we begin to believe are our own.

Life moves quickly and unless we take the time to be in the moment all these thoughts and emotions we have collected can soon fill up our own closet. How many times have we found ourselves wishing we could go back to when we were children? Often that occurs when we are in the midst of feeling pressured in today's world perhaps while under the stress of a job, relationships or financial problems.

For those who did not have a very good childhood, they may wish to go back and do things over. How many times do we say, "If I had known then what I know now…"? The thing we tend to forget is this; we wouldn't have gained the knowledge without going through the growing pains. There is no going back and redoing but there is learning, evolving and growing in mind, body and spirit if only we allow ourselves that luxury and believe we truly do have the power within ourselves to move forward.

Chapter Three

Emotional Hoarding

It didn't take long before the closet was extremely unorganized. Every time Sally opened the closet door, she instantly would see all the dark and dreary undecorated boxes. Without even realizing it, Sally had begun collecting all kinds of emotions and most of them were not happy ones. If she were to take the time and really look at the boxes she would see some were not even her own experiences and memories. The contents of her closet were becoming so jumbled it was almost impossible to tell one from the other: one big mess!

One afternoon Sally decided she really should take a look in that closet and see if she could make room for a few more boxes. After all, she was certainly still experiencing life! There were days that other people would make fun of her for not being the right height, the right weight, too pretty, not pretty enough, dressed too nice, not fashionable enough, or they thought she was too rich, too poor, too quiet or too loud. Sally had friends who she really enjoyed doing things with but there were some in her school who were downright mean to her. Some days Sally felt empowered and other days she didn't feel important at all. Even her family was changing, or was it Sally? Often they would argue about what she should wear, who she should go out with or where she should go. Then there were the family members who made her feel very uncomfortable to be around. She didn't want them to touch her, to look at her or even to speak to her and worst of all she couldn't tell anyone why she felt that way. So she said nothing then people thought she was too shy or too stuck up to take part in the family's activities. What could she say? After all, she carried the secret which she still believed was her fault. Life was getting complicated.

So Sally got to work and began moving the nicer boxes to the front so at least that would be what she would see when she opened the door and threw the dark and dreary boxes in behind them. However, as she picked up a dark box Sally would remember the negative thoughts and feelings associated with it. There were even boxes that when she held them she remembered the feeling but not the experience and there was no way she was opening that box! She found herself becoming upset and angry over things that had happened years ago and it wasn't long before she had enough of this sorting and rearranging and decided just to shut the door and be done with it.

Sally was very surprised that she could hardly shut the closet door. With all of her might, she pushed, and she shoved and she pushed some more until Sally heard the latch go click. She breathed a big sigh, "Ah, I am so glad that is over." She decided right there and then that she would just walk away and never, ever as long as she lived would she open that closet door again...she would be just fine. "That way", she told herself, "I will never remember all the bad memories and never have to feel lonely, sad, hurt or angry again. I will never look at those ugly boxes of negative memories anymore, and that is that! Besides, I don't have time to sort things out. What good does that do anyway?"

So it was that years passed, and Sally never opened that closet door again. She thought she had put all those thoughts out of her head and if one memory did try to slip in Sally instantly shut it down, shook off the feeling and told herself to forget about it. Had she taken a moment to really pay attention to her body when her mind went to those thoughts from the past, she may have realized that there were twinges, pains and aches that would manifest and last some times for days. Could there be a connection? Sally only knew she did not have time to think about it.

What Sally didn't understand was that she had become an emotional hoarder. Not only did she tuck away all of her life experiences, but she had begun collecting the actions, emotions and experiences of others. Could her closet really keep these hidden away forever?

Now more than ever we are constantly being connected to the community, our family and friends and the world at large through the internet. This can be wonderful but what can this really do to us if we don't take the time to disconnect from time to time? Regardless of what we read or see is true or false, once taken in through our senses, our subconscious mind has made a mental note and how it made us feel. If we constantly allow ourselves to take in so much information from other people we can begin to feel lost and uncertain of our own truth. All too often we may begin to repeat what others have said and done without thinking it through or asking ourselves if this information is what we truly believe. Are we making judgments based on other groups' opinions or are we forming our own minds based on what we perceive to be for the higher good of ourselves and others? Perhaps some of our thoughts or actions from the past are weighing heavily on our hearts but we have chosen to hide behind the fear of what others will think of us should they find out. We tuck them away with the belief that if we never mention it again it goes away.

Secrets will burn into our emotional well-being deeper than anything else. They are usually held inside through shame, guilt or fear that was implanted years before. How liberating it is to let the secrets out and to be our authentic selves! By admitting to our secret stories, we find release from years of personal torture and when the time is right

to share these secrets with others, we may be the
one who helps other people to be free.

Then there are the secrets of others that we
choose to carry along our life's journey as well
as our own. There may be situations from our
childhood where we were told not to say anything
with the threat of punishment to ourselves or those
we love. All too often abusive actions are silenced
through the threat of harm through exposure or the
child is made to feel it was all in their imagination
or it was their fault. In these situations, the abuser
has made the abused feel responsible and guilty for
what has happened and thus she would not want
others to know. Too many people have allowed the
words of others to influence their own self-worth
and respect. After awhile the comments of others
begin to feel like a giant earworm that plays over
and over in our minds. If left unchecked we will
begin to believe this to be true. Without realizing it
we will begin to speak about ourselves in this same
negative way and the circle continues of our putting
out negatively and receiving the same back. A part
of us believes that unkind or abusive behavior is
somehow all we deserve. Unfortunately, there is
usually the feeling that others will think less of us

for having spoken out, even though in truth, we have nothing to be ashamed of but we hide behind the fear of what others will think.

One of the hardest but most important steps on our life's journey is to understand that we only have control over what we say and do, not what others say and do. We also are the ones who decide how we will react to the words and actions of others and ultimately how we allow those words and actions to affect us. We can only choose to feel pleasure or pain at one time and choose to live out of love or fear at any given moment in time. There are definitely experiences in life that were the doing of someone else and we had no control over the situation but healing from these actions is in our hands. The emotions we carry are our own. We are the ones in our head and only we can determine how we honestly feel at any given time. As long as we allow the negative energies from past experiences to hide away as secrets, we are allowing these energies to control us.

95% of doctor visits can be traced back to stress related situations. In this "must be busy" world we live in, we are not allowing ourselves to de-stress and in turn, we are creating dis-ease of the body. When the emotions are not dealt with they build up and the only escape is through physical pain in the body and mind. Sleepless nights spent tossing and turning is a very common complaint, which in turn creates its own set of problems. Migraines, tension headaches, back and shoulder pain as well as breaking down of the immune system to mention a few. Overeating can be an attempt to comfort the body through food when we are feeling emotionally deficient. Not eating because of the judgments we have created and the unworthiness we feel causes the body to slowly shut down. Both of these are examples of the mind, body and spirit out of balance. Most often there is an emotional trigger that can be found somewhere at the root of physical pain.

Many have yet to see this connection of mind, body and spirit well-being and think it is a sign of weakness to allow the mind to influence the body, or for depression and anxiety to be hidden behind a smile and a laugh. There is often a feeling that nothing can be done or that it is too late to make changes, this can hold us back from truly finding joy in our life. Too often we do not wish to take the time to sort out whether we are listening to our ego or Higher Self. We find it easier to blame others for our circumstances, our past life experiences, or family life, for how we feel today. A large part of that is true. This all shapes our opinions, our likes and dislikes, even though we hold the power to make changes, we first have to take a deep, long, honest look at ourselves.

Often, we are like Sally and instead of sorting out our closet we pretend everything is in order. And like Sally, one day we will find it harder and harder to keep all those thoughts we have accumulated over the years tucked neatly away in our subconscious mind. In an effort to forget, there will be some of us who will resort to drugs, alcohol or even straight-up denying that there are things in our lives that are upsetting. Others will roll along through life with a smile on their face and pain in their hearts, for they are afraid or too proud to speak of the hurt that is inside. Still, others will go through all the motions of what they were taught makes a good wife, husband, follower of a religion or member of society, when inside they feel as though they are truly fading away, empty and lost. Every one of these people needs to open that closet door and take inventory of what exactly they are storing. More often they will be like Sally and think they can simply close the door to their thoughts and memories and never visit them again. What complications could possibly come from this?

Chapter Four

Denial

The days, weeks and years passed, and Sally grew into a young woman. More experiences came into her life, some good and some not so good. Sally had lived through times of much happiness but also times of great sorrow and pain. There were people who came into her life and brought with them fun and excitement and those who promised these things but only used it to bully her into doing things to please them, not her. Why was she being drawn into these negative relationships? It was as though she was blinded by the hope of getting it right this time or perhaps, she was feeling this was all she deserved. Without realizing it, Sally had slowly begun building a wall around herself to protect her feelings. If she didn't get too close, too involved, then she could keep her secrets and avoid the risk of getting hurt. She thought of it as her castle, her safe place where she could pull up the drawbridge when she didn't want anyone else to come in. What she didn't realize was this fortress not only kept the bad things out but was beginning to hold her captive. How long would it be before the walls come crumbling down?

One night as Sally lay in her big comfy bed, just settling in to think thoughtful thoughts and hoping tonight to be able to dream dreamy dreams she heard a very strange sound. It was coming from her closet! What could it be? The big wooden door began to shimmy and shake, creak and vibrate as though it were coming alive. Slowly, Sally got up out of her big comfy bed and even more slowly made her way over to the closet door and even more slowly yet, placed her now shaking hand on the latch. It had been a very long time since Sally had put any memories in there. She thought it was better to forget the past. In some strange way she thought by locking them away they would magically disappear, and she would never have to face the shadow side of her emotions. As Sally stood silently outside the closet door a fear like no other spread rapidly through every cell of her body. It made her muscles ache, her head spin, and her heart beat so wildly she was certain it would pop right out of her chest onto the floor!

Sally hesitated, what if she didn't like what she saw? How would she deal with it, or would she have to? It was at that moment that Sally realized it had been a long time since she had felt anything at all. Oh, she had good days where she laughed and sang and felt happy, but that spark of joy was long gone. It was as though she couldn't allow herself to be free of her past or worrying about her future. Then there were the secrets? What if she trusted someone so much that she let those out? Thinking these things made Sally decide she could just go back to her bed. Yes, that was what she would do. It was better not to know what was inside that closet; easier not to feel emotions at all. If she didn't feel, didn't think or try to remember then surely everything would be alright. Without giving another thought to what could possibly be happening behind that door, Sally turned to go back to her bed. Although Sally told herself this was the best solution she had a very unsettling feeling deep inside that something was about to happen; something she would have no control over that could very well change her life.

Why did she feel this way? Sally shook her head and decided she must be too tired, and her imagination was running away with crazy thoughts. After all, it was just a closet, what could possibly go wrong?

Oh Sally! What could go wrong indeed? Her higher self was trying desperately to tell her she was missing something as vital as breath in her life but she wasn't listening. How often are we like Sally and ignore our emotional and mental body? Instead of sitting quietly and allowing our true self to speak to us we cover it up with excuses, fears and misguided thoughts. It certainly is not uncommon to have our Higher Self reach out to us during the wee hours of the morning. It is then that we have finally put the conscious mind and physical body to rest and our subconscious is open to suggestions. However, too often we have tossed and turned as our conscious mind relives all the day's events which can lead to reviewing the past regrets, remorse, anger and hurt then moving right along to worrying about the future until we either give in to sheer exhaustion or get up. Too often we may resort to taking medication to aide us in falling asleep or only half rest in front of the TV or computer. Does this really resolve the issue?

Like Sally, many feel that they had hid all their memories, good and bad, or even totally forget about them and thus creating a safe place. However, the truth is our thoughts never really go away. We have to remember them first in order to address them. How we learn to deal with them, accept them for what they were, and learn from them is what is important. Pretending things never happened or didn't affect us really does nothing in helping us find joy and fulfillment in our lives. We give ourselves a false sense of security by creating those walls or as in Sally's case a castle, around us, forgetting that walls not only keep things out but hold us inside as well. A castle can be our safe place or our prison and it all depends on our mindset. 95% of all our daily thoughts are reruns, or in other words the collection of all our past thoughts and memories. That doesn't leave a lot of room for new intake! Similar to Sally's closet, our minds can get extremely overloaded with only 5% of space left in there. There comes a time when we need to examine what we have shoved inside our minds.

Secrets are the greatest burdens we can carry. They hold us back from honest relationships with others, rob us of joy today and prevent us from simply being our authentic selves. The greatest reason we hold onto these secrets so tightly is the fear of what others will think of us. Sometimes it is because we know we have done something unkind or unloving towards someone or we have had something done to us that hurt us deeply but we are afraid we were somehow responsible. This happens most often when there has been bullying or sexual abuse. We may tell ourselves others have had much worse things occur in their lives, so we do not have the right to say our incident is important enough to warrant concern. Perhaps we carry a feeling or belief that was instilled in us at a very young age that we will not be accepted or loved if anyone knew our secret. Guilt can burn a hole in the soul if we let it. It is so important to forgive ourselves and others in order to free the chains that hold us in the past. Every time we bring up the experience and feel the same emotions, we are giving power to the abuser and allowing their words and actions to affect us. Forgiving someone does not mean we have to tell them face to face or go and have dinner with them, but it does allow us to break free of the control that experience has over us. When we can forgive ourselves, we are acknowledging we are bigger and greater than our past. We can look back and learn from those experiences and step forward in our own personal power to change and to evolve. We cannot change what was said or done but we can use our knowledge to break negative patterns so we can shape a future we desire. However, admitting we have fears, secrets and needed forgiveness either in giving or receiving can be the hardest weight to lift from our soul.

What if we were to understand that we cannot feel both pleasure or pain at the same time? Do we really recognize that we are choosing to live in either fear or love in every moment? Perhaps we hide behind the belief that we have no control but rather everything and everyone else is to blame for our so-called failures or losses. We humans are a funny lot aren't we? It is so easy to take the credit for a successful moment in time but oh how we despise being accountable for an error. How we handle both the good and the bad times is completely up to us whether we want to admit it or not. Only we can determine how we feel, think and how we act, ….no one else, bottom line. Should we choose to ignore this and continue to think we have no power, and then we will not have any. Our thoughts become our reality. How we think of ourselves is then relayed to those around us. For example, if we find we are in situations where people are always controlling us and we are always trying to please people we do well to take a step back and look at what is going on here. We feel we cannot say no because we are afraid others will not like us, or we are not doing the "right" thing so we are unknowingly putting that energy out there that says, " I need to be controlled or I need to feel needed and useful." Someone who feels they have to run everything is attracted to this energy and so the cycle begins. Learning to speak our own truth goes a very long way in breaking this type of negative circle.

Sally was no doubt at a crossroads in her life even if she was not totally aware of it. Knowing deep inside that changes were coming and necessary but not totally understanding what they may be. Automatically she went to fear of the unknown and once again found refuge in her castle and pulling up the draw bridge in an attempt to have the feeling pass. Guess what?; Uncertainty and doubt do not disappear but rather grow in intensity if left on their own. Nothing is more consuming to mind and body than indecision. How many sleepless nights are the result of us not making up our minds? As good as it is to weigh all sides in a decision, failing to say nay or yah can lead to a continuous battle in our mind. The stress is not in the actual decision but in the fear of making a wrong one. Once we step up and decide it can feel as though a great weight has been lifted. We are able to focus on moving forward. Should we choose to ignore decision making, all we are doing is allowing the stress to build, build and build inside until such a time when our mind and body say, "NO MORE!"

Chapter Five

The Explosion

So it was, just as Sally had made up her mind to leave the closet and was turning to go back to her big comfy bed, the closet door burst open crashing loudly as it hit her bedroom wall. Boxes came pouring out like a mighty flood; big boxes, small boxes, gray, black and brown boxes. Sally could not move quickly enough to get out of the line of fire. Frozen in time and space, Sally just stood there as all the boxes came at her as though they were attacking her one by one. As each box fell, its lid flew off spilling emotions everywhere knocking Sally to the floor. Sally sat defenseless in the middle of this chaos as her mighty castle, came crumbling down around her. All those plain, ugly boxes that she had allowed to fill her closet were now strewn around her and all over her bedroom floor. What a mess of emotions!

Sally couldn't hold back any longer. Tears began to fall like rain down her cheeks, everywhere she looked were open boxes spilling out their contents of negative emotions. All the sadness, loneliness, bitterness, hurt feelings and anger was piled high around her to the point of almost smothering her. She couldn't stop all the memories from flooding back anymore, eventually, Sally stopped trying and gave into uncontrollable sobbing. She wasn't even sure where some of these things were coming from. Had she really saved so much?

In a last attempt to get things under control, Sally reverted to her way of dealing with things, she closed her eyes tightly hoping to block out what was all around her. It didn't help one bit! She could still see the boxes in her mind's eye no matter what she did and when she opened her eyes, hoping this was just another bad dream, there they were. She tried pushing them away from her but the pain they caused when they hit, could still be felt on her body. It was as though every cell of her being was actually hurting and screaming out in pain from all these boxes. A wave of panic came over her. What if this feeling never went away? Sally allowed that thought to consume her as she slumped to the floor, and the darkness enveloped her.

Over the years, Sally had piled, shoved and crammed many of these boxes into her closet in an attempt to forget. What possible connection would they have on her life today? Why was she feeling emotional and physical pain? Was it just from the boxes hitting her?

How often have we been told to just forget about it and move on? Perhaps we have tried to convince ourselves if we don't think about it, it no longer bothers us. As explained before, our subconscious mind does not work that way. All the data we absorb through all our senses is stored for future use whether we want to acknowledge it or not. Without our being consciously aware of it, these memories are still affecting our thoughts, actions and limitations we put on ourselves. Remember, we carry over 95% of our thoughts from the past into today. Triggers are created in our subconscious mind, so when a certain word is spoken, an action is taken, or a combination of the two happens in our lives, a preprogrammed emotional and physical response occurs automatically. When we refuse to clean out the closet of our mind, we too can have an explosion like Sally did. Often this will result in a breakdown of our mental and/or physical state of well being. It can appear to be extremely overwhelming a task at first, and like Sally, we may try to close our eyes in the hopes it will all go away if we ignore it. Alas, that doesn't work. We may be able to run away from our thoughts for a while; by making ourselves busy, by working long hours, masking our thoughts through addictions, running away from responsibilities or misusing medications. These are all common ways we try to hide from facing the task of dealing with our own mind matter. We may carry on this way for quite some time pretending all is wonderful but in the end, we cannot keep hiding from ourselves. This behaviour only creates more negative life experiences until a decision has to be made; we either create an even larger barrier between us and the rest of the world, or we stop and make changes. It can be difficult to do it all alone. After all, if we have lived most of our lives in denial we may have quite a time sorting through what is reality and what is our imagination. Setting aside our pride and ego is key if we truly wish to roll up our sleeves and get to work empowering ourselves and make changes. Where to begin?

We are the only ones who can truly get into our own heads. No one else's beliefs and actions can affect us unless we allow them to. Another's words may hurt us but only for the moment if we remember we are in control. It is the indecision that leads to stress and dis-ease of our bodies, so understanding this will help us in making decisions sooner than later. How much baggage do we want to carry? How long do we think we can carry the secrets? The energy we use to keep things hidden is far more than allowing ourselves to heal. We can never truly be our complete selves if we are afraid to be all we are meant to be. If now is really the only moment in time we have, do we really want to spend it covering up things from the past, or living someone else's expectations of who they think we should be?

Indecision, doubt and fear can too easily consume our every thought if we allow it to. Whatever energy we create around us is brought back to us. What is it that we desire to have in our life? Surely, we do not wish to live surrounded by sadness and secrets, or guilt and anger, when we have the power to choose and live from joy and freedom, gratitude and love! It is in our darkest moments that we have the greatest opportunities for personal growth. It is during those times when we feel totally exposed, lost and void of light, yet we have the greatest opportunity to make life-changing decisions. Will this be the time we decide that enough is enough and change has to happen, or do we allow the darkness to envelop us and hold us captive in a world of fear and loneliness?

Sally had thought all her negative memories and experiences were safe behind her closet door, neatly wrapped in brown paper. All she had to continue to do was not go there, never open the door again and all would be well. But was it really? Had she been living an illusion created by her own mind? Why was she sobbing? Shouldn't all this have been done years ago? No doubt she was wondering what this all could mean.

The human brain is a complicated pile of gray matter and even though they may all look the same, the thoughts of our minds vary from person to person. That is what makes us so amazing!

Consciousness flows through each of us creating our unique personalities. Our thoughts are like the wind that moves the leaves on the trees as it blows by. We cannot see the wind itself but only the results of its action upon the leaves. So too our thoughts can only be revealed to others through our words and actions. When we hold them inside, they build although no one else knows what is happening. Like the wind that grows silent before a storm, we may seem to be at rest to everyone around us. Then suddenly something happens that triggers the storm within us and like the wind that seems to blow out of nowhere, our words and actions react in an uncontrolled manner. We may find ourselves taking out our anger at loved ones and friends who have no idea why we are so upset. Perhaps a fragrance triggers the memory tucked away in the subconscious mind of a person or place where we were hurt or abused. Even a simple phrase spoken by a coworker can open the gate and release those monsters hiding in the darkness. This may happen once, twice or never. Our bodies may decide they have had enough and shut down, refusing to have the will to get out of bed or walk or eat. Our minds may become so foggy that concentrating on simple tasks is overwhelming and sleep, even though our body craves it, becomes impossible. What if we could use this time to heal, to grow, to let go of what no longer serves us? Can it be done? At the time this happens we too may be like Sally and wonder if this chaos will ever go away.

Chapter Six

The Awakening

Time passed as time tends to do and Sally stayed in her darkness until she could remain there no longer. Through tear-filled eyes, Sally fearfully raised her head slightly, just enough to catch a glimpse of an object on the top shelf of the closet. Something way back in the corner; something long forgotten. At first, she didn't feel she had the strength to face any more boxes and definitely not what they held inside. Maybe she could just stay curled up here for a while longer with her eyes closed and think this through a bit more. After all, things did seem a bit blurry at the moment; confusing to say the least. It was then that Sally wished she could go back to her big comfy bed and dream dreamy dreams. Sally could hardly remember those nights when she felt so free and full of adventure. Was it really that far away and long ago? Would she ever be able to visit that again?

It was at that moment Sally realized there was no going back. She had come this far and now she had to make a decision. She could stay curled up in her own darkness or what? Although Sally had no idea what the other choice was, she did know she didn't want to be so unhappy. Joy had left her, and she wanted it back. All she could think of was to move and then maybe the answer was still in her closet.

It took some doing to stretch her now exhausted body even a little bit. She knew if she ever wanted to see everything that was stored in her closet she would need to find the strength somehow to stand. There was no one else in her room. There was no one telling her what to do. This was up to Sally and Sally alone. She was surprised how much time and actual physical and emotional energy it took to even will herself to move! Finally, after a lengthy dialogue with herself and an even longer, slow breath, she was able to empower herself enough to gently raise her head and open her eyes once more.

That is when she saw them; some beautifully decorated boxes. Pushing the now-empty boxes away from her, Sally managed to create enough space that she could safely stand up. Sally lifted her now shaking arms above her shoulders and by willing her fingertips to stretch just a tiny bit more was just able to touch these colourful boxes. With trembling hands, Sally brought down one of these long-forgotten treasures. What a wonderful surprise when she opened the box! A long lost feeling of total and complete love, enveloped her whole body. *It was warm and soothing like the summer sun. She closed her eyes and took a long, slow, deep breath. That was when she felt it; love in every cell of her body. It was at that moment Sally realized that for a long, long time she had chosen to see only the dark and ugly boxes and by doing so had forgotten all about her beautiful memory boxes; the ones filled with love, hope and joy.*

Sally's closet was filled with so many memories and when it couldn't hold any more, it had to open and let them out. Like so many of us, Sally had not taken care of her closest for many years. Without realizing it, she had chosen to ignore her emotions to the point of denying herself love, joy and hope in her life. In doing so, Sally was closing herself off to so many wonderful experiences and opportunities. Sally was simply existing but not fully living her life.

How often do we turn down opportunities out of fear of what people would say or fear of failure? Relationships are not allowed to grow and blossom out of the fear of being hurt again or lack of trust and commitment. Perhaps like Sally, we hold a deep dark secret from our childhood where we were left feeling unworthy of love, the bad girl if we tell. These secrets can be buried so deep inside that we may not even realize how they are affecting our lives.

Whether we believe it or not all our actions and choices are mostly being guided by our memories of past experiences. When a certain word is spoken, a place revisited, a scent, sound or even a song played on the radio, there is an instant reaction brought forward from our subconscious mind in either an emotional and/or physical response. It all can happen so quickly that we may not even realize what is going on, nor do we understand that we can control these reactions instead of them controlling us. So many times, we embrace the fears and accept them as part of who we are instead of taking the time to ask ourselves why we feel this way? Perhaps it is because we do not completely understand how much our thoughts govern our health, or the ability to manifest what we desire in our lives and the conceived reality of our world. What if we were able to change all this by sorting out our thoughts, learning from our past experiences, and developing a positive approach in all areas of our lives? How could our lives get any better?

More often than not, we choose to take what appears at first to be the easiest route in our decision-making, but in reality, it brings with it much pain. Rather than being open to experience true joy and happiness in our lives, we hide the secrets, the fears, and the low self-esteem behind a fake smile. Unworthiness is a heavy burden that we unnecessarily carry. Usually, this weight has been taken on at an early age. Too often, it has been put upon us when we were children by adults in our family circles or by cultural and religious beliefs. As children, we believe what is told to us and done to us, is what we deserve. What else would we think, especially when we are quite young? After all, our tribe is there to look after us, protect us and show us how to live. It isn't until we are older that we can explore our own truths but only if we are willing to look at all our thoughts.

Sally had hit rock bottom. Physically and mentally, she shut down. She allowed the darkness from her past to swallow her up. It wasn't until she realized that she didn't want to feel like this anymore, that change began to happen. We have the choice to stay down, or get to work raising ourselves back up. It can be painful at first but oh how empowering once we realize that WE are the ones changing our own lives. It all starts with our thoughts and being open to receive the light back into our lives. Darkness does not have power over light, rather darkness is measured by the degree of light it does or does not contain. Therefore, darkness is a lower form of light!

We are worthy and deserving to have love and happiness in our lives. It is within our grasps if only we are willing to reach deep inside and take ahold. No matter how much someone else loves us, is kind to us, encourages us if we do not open our hearts and minds to receiving this love and to awaken our own self-discovery we will remain in darkness. Why should we choose to allow secrets from our past to overshadow all goodness that could be ours today? Everyone on this planet is doing the best they know how at this moment in time and that includes us! We view the world through either pleasure or pain and choose to live from a place of love or fear. When we are in the darkness it may not seem we have a choice, but truly we do! It may seem impossible to think we have any control over our lives when physically and emotionally we are shrouded with such an overwhelming feeling of helplessness that we are literally paralyzed to the point of shutting ourselves off to the outside world. Perhaps we even become unable to get out of bed, to make decisions or to see the goodness anywhere, much less in ourselves. It is in those darkest moments that we can uncover our greatest strengths. Once our secrets and sadness are revealed what can hurt us? This is when self-empowerment takes control to raise us up, but only if we allow it too. Think of all the wonderful causes that have risen after a tragic experience. All the volunteer organizations that serve our communities and those in need are often made up of people who have been down the road of despair and loneliness themselves. They have come to understand how important they can be to someone else by knowing when it is time to share their own stories or when it is time to sit silently holding space with a person in need.

Sally had shut herself off for so long she didn't even know who she really was. Now all her secrets, thoughts, and feelings of every shape and size were all out there in the open for her to see. All those years she thought they were packed neatly away in her closet where no one, including herself, would ever know about them. Surprise! It was her closet and here she was, alone in her room, left to sort it all out. We can never run away from ourselves, can we? Too often we try and hide behind drugs, alcohol, staying alone or pretending to be the life of the party, work all the time, move from one partner to another or job to another or focus on everything in life but ourselves. We may keep a lengthy emotional distance between ourselves and friends, even life partners in order to keep that closet door shut. After all, we have everything under control; out of sight and out of mind right?

Chapter Seven

Moving Forward

Handing herself over to this sensation was both the hardest and easiest thing she had ever done. Sally did not realize just how much she had missed feeling truly loved until this moment. Even though she longed for it there was something inside her fighting to turn it away. Yet right now when she surrendered to the love, it moved so effortlessly through her whole being and brought her such joy she thought of nothing else. What had been stopping her from allowing this to happen? Would she be able to keep it moving through her?

Sally then took a good look at all of the boxes that lay open around her room. There were big boxes, small and tiny boxes, dark boxes and bright boxes. Some had bows, some had tags, some had only an emotion, and they were everywhere! All these memories, all these emotions had been more than Sally could bear. At first, the darkness seemed like a blessing because it blocked all feelings from coming or leaving her. A sort of numbness had come over her and for a brief moment in time, she felt it gave her peace.

Sally didn't know how long she was in a cocoon, but the moment finally came when she knew she had to break out. It was time to return to the light and shed the darkness. Sally could not wait for anyone to do it for her; she had to be the one to break free. During that time of transformation, her emotions seemed to bounce from happiness to sadness, from hope to despair and all it took was a change in her thinking. She could be embracing the memories of a colourful box she had made and truly absorbing all of its love, and then a thought would enter her mind telling her she was not worthy of this love. As easily as the light had shone on her heart, this simple thought swept it away. As she took another look around her room at all the boxes piled high, she had an epiphany.

In that moment she realized she had made all these boxes herself, every last one of them. She was the one who decided what memories to keep, what box they would go in and where it would be placed in her closet. She alone had decided what emotion would be attached to each box just as surely as she was the one who chose its colour and bow. Rather than sorting out her closet and getting rid of some boxes over the years, Sally had decided just to stack, shove, push and cram all these boxes into her closet. She was oblivious to its condition until one day, the closet couldn't hold anymore, and it simply exploded. Had there been warnings? Was she really that blind that she had missed her own feelings? Now that the closet had erupted what was she to do?

Congratulations to Sally for coming out of the darkness! Disguised as a refuge, this seemingly safe place soon transformed into a permanent prison where no feelings come. Loneliness, isolation and despair take over until it seems almost impossible to leave this place. Sally recognized that she didn't like it there and that nothing was going to change unless she made that change.

Too often we allow the ego to keep us a prisoner in our own minds. By repeating messages of unworthiness, anger, resentment and jealousy we keep ourselves from the self-discovery of the truly amazing beings of potentiality that we are. Ego works from fears but our Higher Self is pure love. We choose what voice we listen to and thus whether we live from a place of fear and negativity or from love and positivity. Is it easy to choose? After all, why wouldn't we all want to be open to receive more love and to be more loving? Who would desire to live in turmoil? Perhaps it is our human nature to go back and forth between these two powers within us. Could it be our purpose to explore all possibilities in order to awaken our spiritual evolution while we are here on this planet? Whatever the reason, there are choices we can make on how and what we think. First step is to believe we can make this distinction between whether we choose pleasure or pain, love or fear.

We can see from Sally's exploding closet that it does not serve us well to store too many things. Regardless of how long that closet door was closed, there came a time when nothing could hold it back. As much as we think we can hide things away in our mind, we cannot. They are always there somewhere. If we do not sort things out, either mental or physical dis-ease will manifest to cleanse the body. It is during those times we will be forced to surrender to the darkness so we can recover, rejuvenate and recharge. Even then it is up to us to either except this time as healing or to feel defeated and torn down. We can use the darkness as a warning sign that we need to make changes in our lives. By facing our fears we are able to take back control. If we refuse to make these changes we are handing over our power to our own fears. Guaranteed if we do nothing or if we restack our closet with all the same ideas in time the same results will come around full circle.

It isn't always an easy fix. We may have the same people saying and doing the same things as before and we find we are reacting in the same old manner, however, this time we know how the story ends. It may take a couple of times before we truly understand the connection, but if we are open and more aware of how we see and feel the events in our lives, then we will recognize the warning signs and change how we deal with the situation. We cannot expect our mind and body to react any differently to the same stimuli unless we are willing to change that reaction. The saying, the definition of insanity is doing the same thing repeatedly, and expecting things to change, is fact! All too often we stay in unhealthy and even unsafe relationships out of fear of being on our own, fear of what others would say, fear of what their religious community would think of them if they left, or worse God, or even fear of their lives if they were to go. So they remain going through the same routine, listening for the same slamming doors or broken dishes, screaming insults or times of uncomfortable silence used to embed feelings of loneliness, shame, unworthiness. Then another day comes and we do it all again, thinking today will be different somehow, although nothing has changed but the weather.

Sadness can so easily become part of us that we no longer acknowledge that is how we feel. Our happiness and joy can become so buried beneath its weight that we almost forget what love of life really feels like. How can we know if we never allow ourselves to be all we can be? It takes a lot of work and energy to hide secrets, to pretend to be happy, to look like we are safe, and to put on a false face of self-confidence and an air of well-being when below it all we are filled with our own tears. Then again, some of us may become so good at hiding and pretending that we fool our conscious mind into believing all is well. There may be times when it is easier to conclude we are destined to walk under a dark cloud all our lives than to do soul searching to uncover the secrets that form these thought patterns. Maybe we will spend a lot of our time blaming everyone and everything for how we feel. What if, we were to put all that energy into spinning a positive attitude and creating positive changes? Wouldn't it be wonderful to have that come back into our lives? Wouldn't it be amazing to take off the masks we wear for others and just sit and feel the warmth of the sun and the breeze on our face? What difference would it make if we were comfortable with who we are and accept all things from our life as learning experiences?

Chapter Eight

The Choice is Yours

It became obvious to Sally that she could not leave her boxes the way they were right now. Why, she couldn't even see her comfy bed! Whatever was to be done was all up to her and her choice alone. Was she going to keep all the boxes and try and fit them back into her closet? If that was the answer, would she get frustrated and begin cramming and jamming everything back in like she had before? Would she be able to throw some boxes away? Could she redecorate the boxes? The other choice was to go through each box and decide what to keep, what to throw away or what to re-do. She could take the dark boxes and change them into colourful ones or just let them go. The closet could be full of darkness or colour it was all up to Sally. This would be her choice to make and only she could do it.

All these years Sally had been going through what she thought was an okay life. After all, she really never gave it any thought most of the time. Then, right in front of her, Sally noticed the tiny gray box and she knew right away what was inside. Although it was not very big Sally knew it was made when she was a very young girl after the abuse by her uncle. Funny, Sally thought, how tiny it looked compared to all the others but what an influence it had been all these years. Sally then remembered all the family gatherings she had missed because she was afraid her uncle might show up. She always had an excuse not to go which often upset her parents. She didn't like letting on to them she didn't care about her family, because nothing was further from the truth. There was always the fear that someone would find out and then what? She had friends but no one who knew her dark secret. Even though the incident with her uncle was long in the past it still would haunt her from time to time. There were several times over the years that Sally had thought about telling her mother but then fear would take over and her silence would continue. What would they think of her? So, until today, that tiny gray box had stayed hidden away. Sally knew she needed to revisit this time in her life, no matter how painful in order to cut the cords that had bound her all these years. With this realization, Sally felt a small spark of light awaken in her. What was happening? It wasn't exactly happiness she was feeling but it was much lighter than before. It was as though she had some strength returning to her body and mind.

Sally began to look around the room. Then she raised herself up off the floor and slowly walked around all the boxes. She allowed herself to pick up each box and objectively as possible look at it. Then she would slowly close her eyes, take a deep breath in and experience the emotion attached to each box. At first, she was drawn to the dark and dreary boxes. Initially, their memories were very dark, and holding them was difficult. As time went on Sally understood she had the control to choose what boxes she held and experienced. This discovery gave Sally the strength to let go of many of these memories, at least for the moment. It was during this time that Sally found she was most open to let the love and joy from the beautiful boxes fill her heart and mind.

And so it was that Sally began her journey of closet cleansing. She knew it was not going to be the easiest or the nicest thing she had ever done but deep down in her soul, Sally knew she was worth it. For the first time in a very long time, Sally felt joy and love. She now accepted that she was worthy of these feelings. All these boxes were from her past. They were important to her at one time and helped to make her the person she is today but oh, she could be so much more! If she could think herself into darkness, she would now think herself into the light. Just the thought of it made her smile. Sally had to admit that it was a wee bit scary too. After all, these boxes had been shut away for a very, very long time. She would still have to decide what to do about the secrets, the sadness, and then be open to self-discovery in order to live her life to the fullest.

And with that realization, Sally gently brushed the boxes aside, she had done enough for one night. She would not put any boxes away just yet. Now was the time she would let her mind and body rest. As she looked out her window Sally couldn't help but notice that the moon was full and had risen high up into the night's sky. It had been a long time since she had paid attention to such things. She smiled, pulled back her curtains so its light cascaded across her crisp clean sheets, then snuggled into her big comfy bed. As she closed her eyes, she softly sighed, whispering a wish that only she could hear and allowed the moonlight to envelop her with a blanket of light and love. For the first time in a very long time, Sally went to sleep with gratitude and an open heart looking forward to tomorrow. Tonight, Sally would once again be able to dream dreamy dreams.

Good for Sally! She has taken the first difficult step in sorting out her closet. Indecision is what keeps us captive and living in fear of all the countless "what ifs?" our mind can throw at us. Scenarios that make us crawl back behind our fear of the unknown and locking us away from all that could be. After all, Sally could have chosen to start throwing all the boxes back into the closet without sorting or reviewing any of them. She might have been able to get the door shut again and perhaps it would be years again before she would have to look at what was inside. With this decision she would need to keep hiding secrets, keep herself cut off from all the events she really did want to be part of, in order to avoid seeing certain people who might reveal her secret. The opportunity to add more to her closet, all those amazing positive experiences, would be lost because she would be too afraid to open the closet door. Worse yet, without any warning, the door may come open again on its own. When and where this would happen would be out of Sally's control. This unknown would only add more anxiety to life.

When we look at this story (the closet being our subconscious minds where all our memories are stored from this lifetime and even from previous lives), it is easy to see how everything we have experienced in the past has some bearing on how we act and react today. With that in mind, we can then begin to understand how our actions and thoughts today will affect our reality in the future.

As these memories are tucked away for safekeeping, we decide what emotions are attached to each one so when a similar scenario happens again, we will have programmed our mind and body on how to respond. All the boxes in the closet are these memories and emotions. Wow! Is it a wonder we become jumbled from time to time? How crowded our minds must become with each passing day! With all of our thoughts coming from 95% of our memories, we don't have a lot of space for new ideas, do we? Usually, we clean out our cupboards and closets because we want to make room for something new and to clean and sort things around so we can find things when we want to use them. What if we were to do the same with our thoughts? It is to our advantage that our subconscious stores away things such as how to walk, talk, breathe and the operations of our body. We would have quite a time trying to remember all these things at once on a daily basis! However, there is still a lot of room in that gray matter for other thoughts.

Although we may like to blame other people for how we behave, it really does come back to our choice. We are the only ones who decide which of these thoughts and memories are kept, and where. Do we hold onto negative thoughts, triggering even more negative responses today? Are these negative memories the ones we hold onto and constantly remember and draw from? It may seem a bit crazy that we would want to punish ourselves that way but in fact, we do. Some of us would rather wrap ourselves in sorrow and sadness than go through the process of letting go. Too often, it is the fear of the unknown or exposing ourselves for past deeds that stop us from taking that step forward. Again, the 'what if someone finds out' scenario, overshadows the opportunity to create a positive reality. Is it easy? No, at least not at first. Is it worth it? Most definitely! The power that comes with just making the decision to change and be in control of our lives is enormous. With that decision will come the knowing and belief that we are worthy of a joyful and loving life.

Just like Sally, we may decide to forget about all this, shut the door to our minds and not deal with any of it. Perhaps we would close ourselves off to the point of not allowing positive energy, events or people into our lives so we don't have to feel and deal with anything anymore. Guess what? Just like the closet door, stress will press the body and mind to the point where it cannot deal with it any longer. Whether we like it or not, it will come spilling out in front of us where we will have to do something about it. If we are able to tuck it away again, it will undoubtedly erupt even more violently than before, until we either deal with it or the darkness, often in the form of disease or depression takes over. Stress left unattended will always manifest in physical, emotional or spiritual dis-ease. 85% of all doctor visits can be traced back to stress. Nothing is more stressful than holding onto secrets and working so hard on denying our own thoughts to ourselves! Denying there is anything wrong or needs to be dealt with is a form of indecision. In turn, indecision is constantly searching for a trigger that will open our closet door.

Only we can decide how we feel and how we will react to any given circumstance. Our response can be changed if we are willing to do the re-programming. Simply put, we need to take time to redecorate our boxes. In order to have optimal health, we all need to clean out our closet, dispose of the negatives such as hatred, anger, guilt, remorse and regrets and allow ourselves to truly forgive others and ourselves. By doing so, we are then able to start anew and make room for the positive experiences, love and compassion of others and ourselves. It isn't always an easy job and may even feel overwhelming in the beginning. The first step is to push our ego aside, so we are then free to ask for help. Even to begin to meditate is a way to allow deserved and valuable time for our mind, body and spirit to heal. By objectively looking at our past we can then begin to find out who we are and try new ways of self-empowerment. It can be tough to look at our own lives in a non- judgmental manner but over time, it is possible. It is through self-discovery that we learn from our past, find gratitude and forgiveness of others and ourselves and in that way create the future we desire.

Forgiveness does not mean we will forget an experience but it does allow us to look at it in a new light. We are the ones in control, choosing to take a positive look at what happened and how it can help us today. We are here, now, at this moment and that in itself is something to be grateful for. How we use our memories from the past is totally up to us. Keep in mind whatever energy we put out will be attracted back to us. Should we decide to continue to live in anger and fear that is what we will see in the world around us. What if we were to look instead to the endless possibilities and embrace all opportunities that come to us? Wouldn't it be better for us if we chose to live our lives from a place of gratitude and love? What if through forgiveness we were able to cut the cords tying us to the negative experiences from the past, thus releasing their hold on us today? Why allow those things which have formed fears and secrets in our lives to keep us from living to our fullest today and stop us from creating an even better tomorrow? If we have been able to create this world of negativity then we are able to release all things that no longer serve us and live with endless possibilities. We need to whole-heartedly believe that we are worthy of manifesting and receiving what we desire in our lives.

However, once the closet is cleaned, sorted and organized, we cannot stop there! Oh no! We will need to continue to be ever mindful of our thoughts. It is all too easy to slip back into old thought patterns. Although now, we will recognize the negativity when it attempts to creep in and use our positive mindset to create the reality we want in our life. Once the closet is sorted we don't want it all messed up again, do we? Well, sometimes it may get a bit tossed up. There may be times when a word is spoken, an action taken, even a song on the radio or a scent of cologne can trigger the fears and emotions from the past. The difference now is we know to ask ourselves, "What is causing this emotion in me at this moment in time?" Then, recognizing its origin, the healing process can begin.

We can stay focused on the knowledge we have been through this before and have more experience and knowledge on how to put things in order now. We are the ones in control this time.

Everything begins with our thoughts and we are the only ones who truly feel them and can come to understand them. Taking a few moments every day to sort things out will bring the most reward. Remember, it has taken a lifetime of experiences to shape our thoughts and actions so it can take some time to sort them all out.

Like Sally, we can understand there is only so much we can do at any moment in time. The greatest gifts we can honour ourselves with are patience and kindness in order to heal. We do well to understand that there will be times when we slip back into old ways and habits. The first reaction may be to give up, be hard on ourselves and fill our heads with a sense of self-doubt. However, we have a huge advantage now that we did not have in the past. We know now the past does not have the power to control us, only if we give it permission to. It all starts by taking the power back to decide for ourselves how we feel and how we respond. It is an understanding and accepting that we cannot control the words and actions of others but we do control how we react to the world around us. It is in this way we release our inner strength and ability to create our reality.

On this journey of self-discovery, we will find there are good days and not so good days. We may uncover realities about our own character we are not so fond of and great strengths we had long forgotten. We will learn to be in the moment and there find beauty in ourselves where we had not before. Gratitude and forgiveness will become easier as we feel the cords releasing from the past and the freedom of spirit that can only be discovered in letting go. An acceptance that the most important time is 'this present moment', will guide us to enjoy who we are, where we are and our life experiences. Being loving to ourselves helps us to see that we are all doing the very best we can at any one moment of our lives. We can look back at our experiences knowing we cannot change them, but rather with the mindset of how we can learn from them. By reminding ourselves that worry will only rob us of any joy today and build anxiety for things that have yet to unfold we can then focus on creating in our mind's eye what we truly desire. Remembering the energy we put out will come back to us, we will concentrate on our goals, and being open to opportunities that assist us in manifesting what we desire. Over time we will gain confidence and self-worth. By setting our ego aside we can face our fears, our secrets, and all our sadness and truly begin a path of self-discovery. Life is a journey we agreed to travel with all its ups and downs.

Just as Sally was able to find her safe place, we too can find our comfy bed or place of happiness and contentment, then whisper our own wish for the future, seeing it in our mind's eye, and trusting the Universe to manifest it as we allow ourselves to dream dreamy dreams.

Chapter Nine

What does your closet look like?

One of the hardest steps on our path to self-discovery is simply getting started. Many will read about it, watch videos on it even attend retreats and classes but never actually do the work. Saying we want to feel better, get over something, make changes is all good but unless we truly mean it in our mind, things are not likely to change. First comes the thoughts and mindset, then the words, then the words become actions, and the actions our reality.

Not only does this form of work help tremendously with our personal emotional and physical well-being but also aides with our spiritual growth. Regardless of our personal belief system, we will find optimal health in our life by doing activities that promote mind, body and spirit balance. Part of our purpose on this planet is to experience life. That doesn't mean we all have to be mountain climbers, great scientists or world leaders but it does mean we have an inner desire to discover what our purpose here is all about. Being mindful of our thoughts is key in this balance. After all, we are the only ones in that gray matter 24/7 so doesn't it make sense that we should come to understand ourselves better?

As mentioned previously, it is easy to cast the blame on other people for our lot in life. True, there can be circumstances that because of our age and innocence, we had no control over. Words spoken to us, actions taken against us or even things we observed as children were stored away in our subconscious minds with emotions attached. Often, we react to triggers from these memories today as adults in the same way we did as children; feeling overwhelmed and fearful. Sometimes we may not even realize why we feel the way we do unless we take time to self-examine our thoughts and what they are in this moment in time. Should we allow ourselves to cling to our fears then we will live in fear. The healing process can be extremely difficult, especially if we are not aware at first of the pain's origin. It is not uncommon for us to need help in order to remember those people who were principal players in a painful event. That is where hypnosis and therapy can be most helpful in guiding us gently back in time, to uncover the beginning of our fear and reveal our secrets. Once reviewed, we are now able to look at things from a more objective perspective. In this way, we are able to work on letting go of what no longer serves us and allow the healing process to begin.

Since we can only feel pleasure or pain at any one moment in time and thus live from fear or love, understanding and then releasing our past is vitally important for our transformation into a life of joy. After all, if we are clutching onto something that is causing us pain and fear, then we are allowing it to still control us today. Finding ways to cut the cords that bind us to negativity will free us to be all we desire and deserve to be. It doesn't mean we will completely forget that something ever happened, but we will be in control of how we react to it. Acknowledging it is from the past we can then begin living today. By living in the moment and conscious of how our thoughts create our reality, we are now designing our future. The power of choice and living our life to its fullest is back in our hands.

As mentioned in the previous chapters, our subconscious mind holds all our cell memory from our past and even previous lives, along with how we reacted to these experiences. Automatically our body goes into the same reaction as it did in past similar circumstances and even our emotions can switch in the blink of an eye when these triggers kick in. There are many times when this type of response is necessary for our survival. After all, we wouldn't want to go through the learning process every time we spoke, walked, went to read, rode a bike or drove a car. And we most definitely are grateful that our bodies remember how to breathe, digest our food and all the other bodily functions that go on during our physical life. The problem begins when we have stored responses to negative experiences that will cause emotional or physical pain. For example, when a child grows up in an abusive home whether it is a parent or another relative, emotionally they may have little self-worth and lack of self-respect due to the actions and words spoken to them. Then as they grow and wish to have a relationship themselves it can be very difficult. Certain words spoken, a simple touch, even an innocent gesture by the other person can trigger an automatic emotional and physical response. Over time, they may settle for someone who is not treating them with compassion and love because they do not feel they deserve anything better. Until they clean out their closet and deal with the hurt and mistrust that has been building up in there, happiness will be fleeting. They will be waiting for something bad to happen, a trust to be broken, before they leave or worse yet, they will feel this is as good as it's going to get and settle for a bad relationship rather than being alone.

A comfort zone is not always a good place to be. It can quickly turn into a prison. The fear of the unknown outside of this place can keep someone in a very bad situation. Emotional abuse is just as damaging as physical abuse because it worms its way into the abused person's mind until they begin to believe what they are being told is the truth. It is imperative that the cords to this mindset be cut in order to bring change. As long as there is an attachment the abuser will also have control. Break this bond and a new freedom is born that will open so many opportunities. Even if there is a physical separation between the abuser and the abused, if the emotional attachment is not severed it will remain difficult if not impossible for change to occur.

Remaining afraid of what others may think of us, the fear of being rejected or alone can be difficult hurdles to overcome but they are not impossible! Surrounding ourselves with positive and supportive people who can lift us up instead of putting us down is vital. This can mean leaving the circle of "friends and family" we are presently involved with or in the very least being selective of the time and energy we put into their drama. Seeking the help of others who have gone through changes similar to ours can be extremely helpful. It is through heartfelt conversations that we can discover we are not alone! Someone else has paved the way for us to follow. Be mindful, however, that the path you choose be positive and for the higher good of all and one that gives you strength and courage to move forward.

If we continue to do things the same way what can possibly change? After dropping our white shirt in a mud puddle would we then attempt to wash our shirt in the same mud puddle and expect it to come out clean? What happens if we keep putting the shirt back in the puddle over and over again? It begins to get dirtier and dirtier no matter how hard we want it to be clean! Excepting things to change while repeating the same pattern cannot solve the problem. Continuing to hide the secrets will only hurt us by feeding our fears. We will end up building walls around our lives to keep the secrets in, but they also serve to keep others out. Living with abuse only strengthens the abuser. Holding onto painful memories will only serve to hold us captive and to keep us believing we are the victim. It can be difficult to take down the walls we have built around ourselves. Like Sally, we started out using this protection to save ourselves from heartache but one day, we discovered we have lost more than we have gained. We built the wall, and we are the only ones who can take it down. Finding the one supporting stone and removing it can bring the whole thing down at once. Other times we need to take it down brick by brick until we have all the barriers removed. We will begin to feel strength when we take that first step in empowering ourselves and removing those experiences, memories and often times people that no longer serve us.

Chapter Ten

Steps to healing

The path to healing begins by asking ourselves the three soul questions:

Who am I?
What is it I desire?
What is my purpose?

By doing so we can delve deeper within our own mind to understand and connect to our Higher Self and true purpose. The answers to these simple questions determine everything about us: our thoughts, actions, and our outlook on the world around us and also how we see ourselves. It is surprising how many people are afraid to ask these questions. Perhaps it is the answers that scare us. What if we don't have an answer? Is one more right than the other? What if we don't like the answer we hear? After all, once we know, we know and there really is no going back to our old way of thinking, denying and keeping secrets. We can try but it will get harder and harder to keep pretending and holding everything in not to mention how very emotionally and physically exhausting keeping up a charade really is!

That idea of introspection can be scary, but it can also be the most liberating thing we ever do. After all, we are the only ones who really know what thoughts we have rambling around in our mind; even if we ourselves have little to no idea what they mean! We have to start with a thought and that to some can be overwhelming. Which one of the 80,000 thoughts running through our brain every day is the one that needs to be dealt with? Have no fear that is where asking the three soul questions comes into play. Since they are so very important in helping us on our spiritual journey it only makes sense to take the first step with them.

Are you ready to do your own self-exploration? There is no judgment only empowerment. All the exercises will begin the same with relaxation and simple visualization techniques to assist you and connecting to your inner voice - your Higher Self. You will also need a journal or notebook to use for these exercises. This will be for your eyes only at least for now. You want to be sure you are answering the questions honestly and how you feel at this moment in time. You may wish to share them with someone at a later date but that will be up to you.

Here are a few helpful tips to make these exercises the most beneficial for you.

1- If possible, set up a time and place where you will work through the following exercise daily.
2- No TV, phones or computers on to distract you. This is your time to connect with your true self.
3- If you feel you would like some soothing music that is okay if it is softly playing in the background and you are not tempted to stomp your feet and clap your hands along with it. Spa type or meditation music is fine.

4- Don't rush. Give yourself time for reflection. Remember there are no right or
wrong answers.

5- You will find it beneficial to go over
these exercises from time to time as you
continue to work through "stuff" that
surfaces in your life.

Exercise 1: Who Am I?

In your journal write across the top of a fresh page
the first question, "who am I?" That wasn't hard now,
was it? These three little words seem so innocent
but hold so much power. How you answer these
questions will determine how you see yourself and
in turn how others see you.

Now, if you are ready, begin by making yourself
comfortable.

- Close your eyes.
- Focus on your breathing by saying to
yourself, "I am breathing in." Now take a
long, slow, deep breath in.

- As you are exhaling say to yourself, "I am breathing out." Then slowly exhale, feeling your body relax.
- Do this at least five times, allowing your breath to relax your mind and body.
- Now, ask yourself the first question, "Who am I?"
- Listen to the very first thing that comes to you.
- Without judgment, hear it and be aware of how your body feels when you do.
- Take a few more breaths.
- Open your eyes and write down the answer to this question.
- Write down the following question: "How does this answer make me feel emotionally?" Mention if this surprises you or not.
- Next question: "Do I feel I am more than this?" Why do you feel you are or not?

The answers to these questions can and should change over time as you evolve and grow. As you continue to do these exercises, you will see how your answers to the questions shapes your own opinion of yourself. In turn, what you put out about yourself to the world around you is what others see as well. For example, if you answered, "I am an accountant. (or whatever career choice you are in)" that would indicate you feel and see that as being the most important aspect of who you are. No doubt how you dress, act, people you associate with and places you go, would be based on this answer. You want others to see you like this as well. What if you retired or were laid off? Who would you be then? Similarly, if you are a parent and see yourself as only that, what happens when the children leave home? Do you cease to be someone? Too often people will remain in a bad marriage because they can only identify themselves as a husband or wife and the thought of not being that terrifies them. These are all parts of your learning experience but they are not who you truly are.

Here is another exercise that you can work through to help you to see this. It can take some doing but well worth it. You will no doubt need to repeat this quite a few times but that is perfect! It is like peeling back layers to get to the core. You will be using some visualization for this exercise.

Exercise 2: The Bag

- Close your eyes.
- Focus on your breathing by saying to yourself, "I am breathing in." Now take a long, slow, deep breath in.
- As you are exhaling say to yourself, "I am breathing out." Then slowly exhale, feeling your body relax.
- Do this at least five times, allowing your breath to relax your mind and body.
- Now imagine there is a large clear bag sitting in front of you and in the bag is a swirling purple light.
- You are able to place all your personal belongings into this bag – your clothes, furniture, car, even your house, jewelry, anything material into this bag and watch as it swirls around with the purple light.
- Now you put into the bag all your family and friends.
- Now put your name into the bag and what that means to you. Be sure to put in there any titles or designations you have earned into the bag as well as any degrees and such

- Put your job, career, and volunteer work, anything you do outside of the home.
- Put your beliefs, your judgments into the bag.
- Put all your past secrets, negativities, anything and anyone you feel has harmed or treated you badly into the bag.
- Put your hairstyle, the clothes you are wearing, makeup and allow yourself to see them all swirling in the bag.
- Finally, step into the bag...your full body in there with everything else and watch it all swirl around.
- How does this make you feel?
- There is one important thing to note. You are observing everything outside of this bag. You are so much more than the clothes you wear, the people you are around, the job you do or the processions you own.
- Bring your awareness back to your breath. Taking in three deep breaths.
- Open your eyes.
- Write in your journal how you felt for each item that you placed in the bag. How important were they to you?

- Did you have trouble putting anything in the bag? Did you keep some things out of the bag?
- Could you imagine yourself without any of these things?

The important point of this exercise is to help you to realize that you are a spiritual being in a physical body. All these things you were asked to put in the bag are things you can now look at and decide if they are for your higher good or are they things that should be released? You have chosen to keep these things and only you can know or decide what to let go of. How they make you feel is key. Be sure to record how you felt emotionally as you were doing this exercise as well as any physical feelings.

Exercise: What is it I desire?

Answering this question may seem simple at first. After all, we all have wants and needs in our daily lives. For many people, money is the immediate answer. If we are poor, money can pay our bills, put a roof over our head and feed us. If we already have these things, perhaps money will buy us status and

fame. Again, peeling back the layers is important so
we can find the root of our desires. In these examples,
will money be the solution if we make no other
changes in our lives, or will it only be a temporary fix
leaving us continuously in want of something? Will
being popular bring us joy or are we really looking
for acceptance of others to provide us with self-worth?

Select a new page in your journal and write,
"What is it I desire?" across the page. Look at it
and read it out loud two or three times, letting the
questions sink in. Make yourself comfortable.

- Close your eyes.
- Focus on your breathing and take a long,
  slow, deep breath in.
- As you are exhaling say to yourself,
  "What is it I desire?" Then slowly exhale,
  feeling your body relax.
- Do this at least five times, allowing your
  breath to relax your mind and body.
- Now allow the answer to this question,
  "What is it I desire at this moment in
  time?" come to you.
- Do not judge or question your responses
  but simply let them flow into your mind.

- Be conscious of how these answers make you feel.
- How do you feel emotionally and physically when you think about what you desire? Remember this.
- Ask yourself why you desire this? What is the root emotion that is attached to the desire?
- Bring your awareness back to your breath.
- Do three more deep breaths, with your last exhalation as a sigh.

Now it is time to record your experience to this exercise in your journal being mindful to write how you felt emotionally and physically down. Remember there is no right or wrong. Be honest.

What you desire today may be different tomorrow and the next day. That is okay! It is always important to take the first answer a few steps further in order to get to the root of what it is you truly desire in your life. Often the answer or opportunity will come to you in a very different form than what you first thought would provide you with what you desire. You may need to address some inner fear in order to be in a position to accept what you desire fully into your life.

In the previous example money is a temporary fix but it does not look at a solution. If the fear of what others think is at the root, then we would need to examine why we feel this is needed? Do we love ourselves? Are we still hiding secrets? It is okay not to have all the answers at once, but we do need to ask ourselves these questions in order to be living from a place of love and joy and not from fear and pain.

Exercise: What is my purpose?

This must be the one question we all ask ourselves throughout our lives. Why am I here in the first place? Usually, this question is spoken in times of stress and confusion and out of frustration. Especially during those times in our lives when we thought we had things all figured out then something goes wrong…or at least what we perceive to be wrong happens. We are left with wondering what our purpose is here on this planet.

The wonderful news is we all have a reason to be here. Every single thing we do affects not only our lives but the lives of those around us. Taking a moment to show compassion by helping someone with their grocery bags, smiling and saying hello, donating to a charity, a simple phone call to check in on someone who is ill are all ways that love and compassion are spread through our community. We never really know the effect we make in someone's life but we truly do make a difference. It is through discovering what brings us joy and then living that in our lives, that we soon find our passion and purpose.

It is hard to be genuine if we are hiding behind secrets and fears. The first step in discovering our true path is to be brave enough to take down the walls we have built around ourselves. Bit by bit we unfold our life's contract and begin fulfilling our purpose. We may even find out that we have been traveling the right path all along. There are many lessons we need to learn on this road of life and time and patience are often the teachers. We do well to remember that life is about the journey and all the experiences we have along the way. There really is no right or wrong choices just simply options we have in creating our own unique story.

The people we meet, the choices we make and the thoughts we create all contribute to our life experiences and our version of reality. At the core of this marvelous adventure lies our purpose. It is based on 'love of ourselves' and serving others in a way that is for the Higher Good of all. When we allow our fears to get in the way that is when we are blocked from living our lives to the fullest.

Let's see what the following exercise reveals to you. Again, make yourself comfortable and on a new page in your journal write the question, "What is my purpose?" across the top.

- Close your eyes.
- Focus on your breathing and take a long, slow, deep breath in.
- As you are exhaling say to yourself, "What is my purpose?" Then slowly exhale, feeling your body relax.
- Do this at least five times, allowing your breath to relax your mind and body.
- Place your hand over your heart chakra (energy centre located in the centre of your chest).
- Take another long, slow, deep breath.
- Think of all the things you are grateful for in your life. All the blessings you have at

this moment. Even if it doesn't feel like things are going right, give thanks for your breath and this moment.

- Now be aware of how your body feels as you express this gratitude and allow it to spread to every cell of your being.
- Now with this sense of gratitude still flowing through you think of something that brings you joy and experience how that makes you feel.
- Once more ask the question, "What is my purpose?" and listen without judgment to the answer that comes to you.
- Sit quietly for a few moments.
- Take a few more long, slow breaths in and out.
- Open your eyes.

As you have done in the previous exercise, record everything you experienced in this time of reflection. You may be surprised at what was revealed to you or totally confused! Both are perfectly okay. The main thing is to trust all will be revealed as time goes on and simply record your experiences for now. It is not uncommon that ideas and images will appear to you as you are journaling. That is why writing things out is so important. Remember time and patience are your teachers and there is no fighting them so relax and enjoy the ride!

Chapter Eleven

Keeping a Clean Closet

Regardless of whether we are feeling trapped in our own fears or if we think our life is flowing effortlessly it is vital that we keep track of our mind's "closet" inventory. Otherwise, there will come a time when we will be like Sally; paralyzed emotionally with all our memories, fears and secrets piled up around us. It is during such times that we will be forced to either face the truth or attempt to shove everything away again. Every time the closet door burst opens it gets harder to keep things in. Why not begin de-cluttering now so we are better equipped in designing our reality? Wouldn't it make more sense to discover our purpose rather than living someone else's truth?

Review chapter ten often as you will find those exercises will assist you in evolving and learning more about yourself. This will empower you to freely step into your own truth. You will grow and become all you were meant to be.

Your answers to the three soul questions will evolve as you become more willing to receive the answers. All things are done in Universal time. Do not hold onto regrets of the past but rather take a positive lesson from the experience no matter how difficult it may seem at first. The objective is to release what no longer serves your Higher Good so you can cut the cords to all things that are holding you captive to the past.

Try these simple yet powerful daily rituals to keep your closet in order.

Begin every morning and end each day with a moment of gratitude. Be thankful for something, anything, regardless of how big or small.

- Remember to focus on the positive as the energy we put out comes back.

- Keep your journal for the exercises here and be sure to update your progress even if it just a short note or point form comment. Especially if you need to vent or release negativity. Better out of the mind.

- Take at least 12-15 minutes each day to meditate. The exercises in chapter 10 are all a form of meditation. Doing deep breathing alone can relax the body and mind and assist in releasing stress as well as bringing clarity and focus to mind, body and spirit.

- You may wish to write out a positive affirmation and carry it with you so you can pull it out and read it throughout the day. Keep it simple and positive...no negative words. For example, you may wish to use one or all of these:
    o "I am worthy to give and to receive love."
    o "I have the right to speak my truth."
    o "I will show others kindness and I deserve the same."

- Above all else, show love and compassion to yourself. You deserve it! Love yourself and others will see that beautiful spirit and love it too.

Don't be disappointed if your closet gets a bit cluttered from time to time. Now you know how to sort things out and get it back in order. You cannot control what others say or do but you can control how you react and act. Focus on being the best you can be and trust the Universe has your back. You are here to experience life and to live it to its fullest in whatever way is your purpose.

You are a beautiful being of light that chose to come here at this moment in time to shine. Allow yourself to clean out your closet of all the secrets and the sadness you have stored there and write your own story of self-discovery.

Namaste

About the Author

Rev. Janice Chrysler is an ordained Metaphysical Minister, Reiki Master, Certified Hypnotherapist, Intuitive Spiritual Coach and author. She has designed, written and presented a variety of seminars and workshops which specialize in helping others on their road to self-discovery. Through these private and group sessions, she has assisted others in awakening spirituality in all aspects of their lives.

Rev. Janice is also an approved teacher on Insighttimer.com where you can listen to her guided meditations. She can be booked for speaking or facilitating engagements, when she's not performing a Wedding, Naming, or Celebration of Life service!

To learn more about Rev. Janice Chrysler, Ch and Mindful Journey services visit:
http://mindfuljourney.ca/
www.Facebook.com/Mindful-Journey

Services
by Rev. Janice Chrysler

Hypnosis Sessions:
- Spiritual Coaching
- Journey of the Soul

Workshops and Seminars:
- Mind, Body and Spirit orientated
- Reiki Levels 1,2,3 and Masters
- Beyond the Chakras
- The Goddess Speaks
- The Path to Self-Discovery Series
- Make It Happen
- Speaking engagements, full day or week-end retreats

Intuitive Readings:
- In person
- Email
- Zoom or Facetime

Mindful Journey Publishing:
- Make It Happen…Motivation, Meditation, Manifestation
- The Goddess Speaks Oracle Cards
- Beyond the Chakra Oracle Cards
- Make It Happen Oracle Cards
- Light, Love and Healing Oracle Cards

Made in the USA
San Bernardino, CA
11 June 2020